Circus! Circus!

POEMS SELECTED BY

Lee Bennett Hopkins

ILLUSTRATED BY

John O'Brien

ALFRED A.
KNOPF
New York

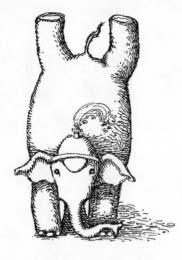

For Eileen Tway,
who teaches
the love of poetry
in *every* way. L B H

For Drew J O B

This is a Borzoi Book published by Alfred A. Knopf, Inc.

Text copyright © 1982 by Lee Bennett Hopkins
Illustrations copyright © 1982 by John O' Brien
All rights reserved under International and Pan-American
Copyright Conventions. Published in the United States
by Alfred A. Knopf, Inc., New York, and simultaneously in
Canada by Random House of Canada Limited, Toronto.
Distributed by Random House, Inc., New York.
Designed by Mina Greenstein
Manufactured in the United States of America
10 9 8 7 6 5 4 3 2 1

Library of Congress Cataloging in Publication Data
Main entry under title: Circus! circus! (Knopf juvenile)
Summary: Includes eighteen short poems about the
circus and its performers, with illustrations.
1. Circus—Juvenile poetry. 2. Children's poetry, American.
[1. Circus—Poetry. 2. American poetry—Collections]
I. Hopkins, Lee Bennett. II. O'Brien, John, 1953- ill.
PS595.C53C5   811'.008'0355   81-20932
ISBN 0-394-85342-3   AACR2
ISBN 0-394-95342-8 (lib. bdg.)

ACKNOWLEDGMENTS

Every effort has been made to trace the ownership of all copyrighted material and to secure the necessary permissions to reprint these selections. In the event of any question arising as to the use of any material, the editor and the publisher, while expressing regret for any inadvertent error, will be happy to make the necessary correction in future printings.

Grateful acknowledgment is made to the following for permission to reprint the copyrighted material:

Atheneum Publishers, Inc., for "To A Circus Acrobat" from *Catch Me A Wind* by Patricia Hubbell. Copyright © 1968 by Patricia Hubbell.

Curtis Brown, Ltd. for "The Ringmaster" by Lee Bennett Hopkins. Copyright © 1982 by Lee Bennett Hopkins.

Doubleday & Company, Inc., for excerpts from *People I'd Like To Keep* by Mary O'Neill. Copyright © 1964 by Mary O'Neill. Reprinted by permission of Doubleday & Company, Inc.

Margaret Hillert for "Circus Fare." Used by permission of the author who controls all rights.

Bobbi Katz for "At the Circus" and "When All the Crowds Are Gone." Used by permission of the author who controls all rights.

Little, Brown and Company for the selection from "The Big Tent Under the Roof" from *Verses from 1929 On* by Ogden Nash. Copyright 1936 by Ogden Nash. By permission of Little, Brown and Company.

Mrs. Gifford M. Lloyd for an excerpt from "Such Things are Far Away" from *The Ancient Beautiful Things* by Fannie Stearns Davis Gifford.

Contents

from SUCH THINGS ARE FAR AWAY

The circus comes this week!
And there might be a skating bear,
And white Arabian horses there;
And pop-corn, and balloons,
Gold, purple, scarlet moons,
And great wise elephants,
And dogs that count and dance.
And cow-boys! We shall see!

Fannie Stearns Davis

from THE BIG TENT UNDER THE ROOF

Noises new to sea and land
Issue from the circus band.
Each musician looks like mumps
From blowing umpah umpah umps.

Odgen Nash

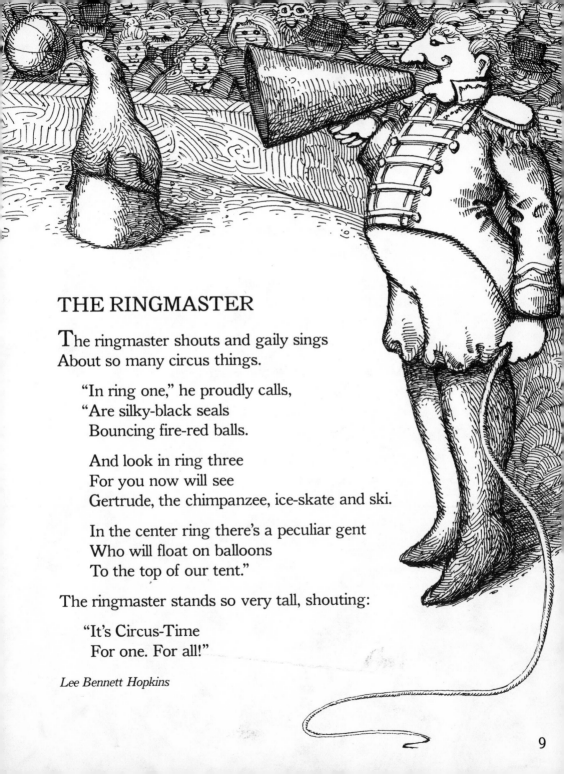

THE RINGMASTER

The ringmaster shouts and gaily sings
About so many circus things.

   "In ring one," he proudly calls,
   "Are silky-black seals
     Bouncing fire-red balls.

   And look in ring three
   For you now will see
   Gertrude, the chimpanzee, ice-skate and ski.

   In the center ring there's a peculiar gent
   Who will float on balloons
     To the top of our tent."

The ringmaster stands so very tall, shouting:

   "It's Circus-Time
     For one. For all!"

Lee Bennett Hopkins

9

from CIRCUS

I tame the very fiercest beast,
the lion, proud and wild,
but I don't fear him in the least,
for me he's meek and mild.

I step into the lion's cage,
he bares his fearsome fangs,
but let him rave and rant and rage,
I feel no fearful pangs.

I boldly stare into his face,
his roar is harsh and loud.
I clasp him in a strong embrace
before the awe-struck crowd.

And when I calmly place my head
between his gaping jaws,
I fear no fear, I dread no dread,
I only hear applause.

The mighty lion wants to please
and so does all he can
because he knows, because he sees
that I'm a fearless man.

Jack Prelutsky

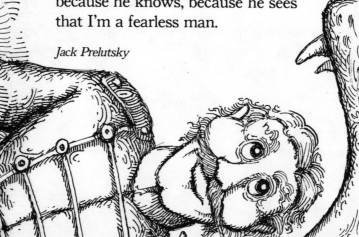

CIRCUS FARE

Pink cotton candy
And purple-urple pop.
(A clown came running through the ring
And did a belly flop.)

Popcorn and peanuts,
A hot dog on a bun.
(A lady walked a tightrope
And we clapped when she was done.)

Ice cream and lemonade,
Apple on a stick.
(A man between two horses
Did a very fancy trick.)

Pizza and French fries
And frozen yogurt, too.
(Green fire edged a hoop
With a tiger leaping through.)

Pink cotton candy
And chocolate cigars.
My tummy's full of rainbows
And my head is full of stars.

Margaret Hillert

TOO MUCH TO SEE

There's too much action for only two eyes—
Too many fun things so full of surprise!

I'm missing so much! But what can I do?
I wish I had ten eyes instead of just two!

Solveig Paulson Russell

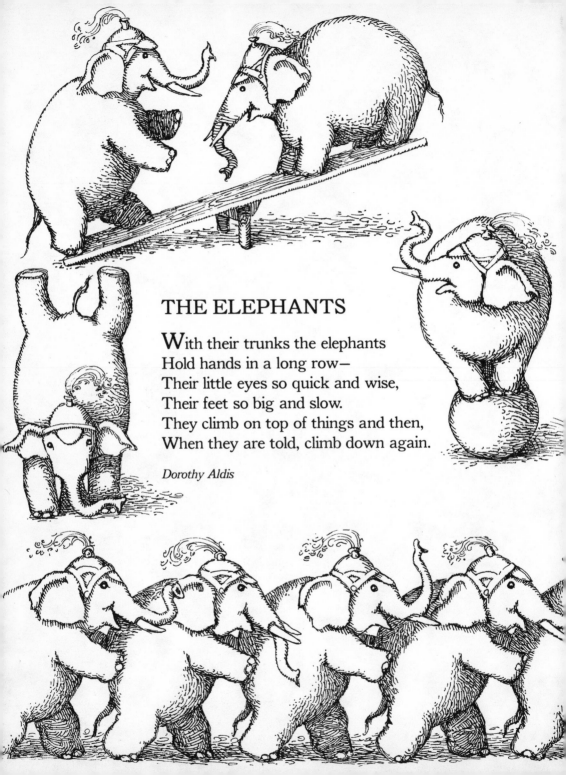

THE ELEPHANTS

With their trunks the elephants
Hold hands in a long row—
Their little eyes so quick and wise,
Their feet so big and slow.
They climb on top of things and then,
When they are told, climb down again.

Dorothy Aldis

CIRCUS ELEPHANT

Does the Elephant remember,
In the gray light before dawn,
Old noises of the jungle
In the mornings long gone?

Does the Elephant remember
The cry of hungry beasts;
The Tiger and the Leopard,
The Lion at his feasts?

Do his mighty eardrums listen
For the thunder of the feet
Of the Buffalo and Zebra
In the dark and dreadful heat?

Does His Majesty remember?
Does he stir himself and dream
Of the long-forgotten music
Of a long-forgotten stream?

Kathryn Worth

from CORCUS

The high-diver climbs to the ladder's top
and gazes down—a long, long drop.
She flexes and prepares to go
into the waiting tub below.

With perfect poise, the diver plunges
into the bathtub, stuffed with sponges.
She lands! The sponges slish and slosh.
What a peculiar way to wash.

Jack Prelutsky

TO A CIRCUS ACROBAT

Up!
Leap!
Quick,
Call me,
Bright one!
Reach out your hand
From your high trapeze
And signal me
My name.
My name!
I'll leap
And fly
My crowded bench
To join you there!
We'll slowly turn,
Revolve on wire,
And gaze below us
At the crowd
Of astonished children,
Popcorn-patterned.
And I!
Invincible
And fairy-winged,
Spun on a silver thread.

Patricia Hubbell

THE CLOWN

I like to see
The spotted clown
Throwing dishes
In the air.
When they've started
Coming down
He looks as though
He didn't care,
But catches each one
Perfectly,
Over and over,
Every time,
One and two and
One-two-three—
Like a pattern
Or a rhyme.

Dorothy Aldis

18

AT THE CIRCUS

White horses appeared in a cloud of magic mist,
As if some wizard willed them into being—
Transforming racy white clouds into beasts
That gallop anywhere,
Even across the skies!
Around the ring they go,
Faster than the wind—

Roaring,
         Snorting,
                  Tossing their noble heads!

Slowly, the lights go on,
And they are horses—
Just white horses—
Performing at the ringmaster's command.

My friend lets go of my arm.
He was holding it so tightly.
And we remember to eat our popcorn.

Bobbi Katz

from CIRCUS

The circus people that I see
Are not like me.

They wear spangles on their clothes
And they dangle by their toes
And there is even one who goes,
—and that's the best of all—

Zoom boooooming through a cannon.
She's a human cannon ball.

Beatrice Schenk de Regniers

from THE CIRCUS PEOPLE

...In the first beginning of night
We short-cutted home...
And saw a wonderful sight:

The girl that swung from the high trapeze
Up to the scary heights
Sat on the steps of a caravan
Mending her spangled tights.

The Strong Man hung
A shirt to dry,
And the Tallest-Man-in-the-World
Walked by.

Across the tents
Tree lights were strung
The circus supper
Had begun.
Acrobats and clowns
And kings
Were eating ordinary
Things:
Hamburgers and
Lima beans,
Buttered buns and
Turnip greens. . . .

Mary O'Neill

WHEN ALL THE CROWDS HAVE GONE

What are you like underneath your mask,
When all the crowds have gone?
Do you take off your smile for a little while,
When all the crowds have gone?
Do you always make jokes for the circus folks?
Do you quietly keep to yourself?
What are you really like, Mr. Clown,
When all the crowds have gone?

Bobbi Katz

EPILOGUE

Nothing now to mark the spot.
But a littered vacant lot;
Sawdust in a heap, and there
Where the ring was, grass worn bare
In a circle, soft and brown,
And a paper hoop the clown
Made his little dog jump through,
And a pygmy pony-shoe.

Rachel Field

from CIRCUS

I went to the circus
Now any night in bed
I can see a circus...
in my head.

I can smell the circus smell.
I can see the circus sights
and dizzy razzle-dazzle
of the circus lights.

Beatrice Schenk de Regniers

LEE BENNETT HOPKINS is the editor of numerous highly acclaimed children's poetry anthologies, including *And God Bless Me; Elves, Fairies, & Gnomes;* and *Go to Bed!*, all published by Knopf. He has written a variety of professional texts and articles, and holds advanced degrees from Kean College of New Jersey, Hunter College, and the Bank Street College. Mr. Hopkins lives in Scarborough, New York.

JOHN O'BRIEN has illustrated several children's books, including *Flapdoodle* and *Favorite Tales of Monsters and Trolls*. His illustrations have also appeared in *Cricket Magazine*. Mr. O'Brien, who holds a Bachelor of Fine Arts degree from the Philadelphia College of Art, now lives in Maple Shade, New Jersey.